# XTREME RACES
# RENO AIR RACES

BY S.L. HAMILTON

# Visit us at
# www.abdopublishing.com

Printed in the United States of America, North Mankato, Minnesota.
102012
012013

 PRINTED ON RECYCLED PAPER

Editor: John Hamilton
Graphic Design: Sue Hamilton
Cover Design: John Hamilton
Cover Photo: Corbis
Interior Photos: AP-pgs 6, 23 & 27 (middle & bottom images); Corbis-pgs 1 & 20-21; Dennis
Gray-pgs 2-3, 8, 9, 10, 14-15 & 32; Getty Images-pg 24 (bottom); Joshua Martes-pg 24 (top);
Keith Breazeal-pg 25 (middle); Robert Rooman-pgs 6-7; Tim O'Brien-pgs 4-5, 11, 12, 13,
16-19, 22, 25 (top right & bottom right) & 28-29; U.S. Air Force-pgs 26 (bottom), 27 (top) &
30-31; U.S. Navy-pg 26 (top); Victor G. Archer-pg 25 (top).

ABDO Booklinks
Web sites about Great Races are featured on our Book Links pages. These links are
routinely monitored and updated to provide the most current information available.
Web site: www.abdopublishing.com

Cataloging-in-Publication Data

Hamilton, Sue L., 1959-
 Reno Air Races / S.L. Hamilton.
  p. cm. -- (Xtreme races)
Includes index.
ISBN 978-1-61783-696-1
1. National Championship Air Races--History--Juvenile literature.  2. National Championship
Air Races--Juvenile literature.  I. Title.
797.5--dc23
                              2012945703

# TABLE OF CONTENTS

Reno Air Races . . . . . . . . . . . . . . . . . . . . . . . . . . . . . . .4

History . . . . . . . . . . . . . . . . . . . . . . . . . . . . . . . . . . . .6

Classes . . . . . . . . . . . . . . . . . . . . . . . . . . . . . . . . . . . .8

Qualifying . . . . . . . . . . . . . . . . . . . . . . . . . . . . . . . . . .14

The Start . . . . . . . . . . . . . . . . . . . . . . . . . . . . . . . . . .16

The Course . . . . . . . . . . . . . . . . . . . . . . . . . . . . . . . . .18

The Rules . . . . . . . . . . . . . . . . . . . . . . . . . . . . . . . . . .20

Dangers . . . . . . . . . . . . . . . . . . . . . . . . . . . . . . . . . . .22

Top Pilots and Planes . . . . . . . . . . . . . . . . . . . . . . . . . . .24

Traditions . . . . . . . . . . . . . . . . . . . . . . . . . . . . . . . . . .26

The Finish . . . . . . . . . . . . . . . . . . . . . . . . . . . . . . . . . .28

Glossary . . . . . . . . . . . . . . . . . . . . . . . . . . . . . . . . . . .30

Index . . . . . . . . . . . . . . . . . . . . . . . . . . . . . . . . . . . . .32

# RENO AIR RACES

Pilots and planes from around the world make Nevada's skies their raceway each September during the National Championship Air Races. Commonly called the Reno Air Races, skilled aviators soar across the Nevada desert in a thrilling display of speed and expert flying ability.

*XTREME FACT – The Reno Air Races are also called "The World's Fastest Motorsport."*

*A Corsair takes off at the blue-and-white checked home pylon to begin a race.*

# HISTORY

Nevada rancher and pilot Bill Stead organized the first air race at the Sky Ranch Airfield in 1964. The dirt airstrip was located just outside of Reno, Nevada. This was the start of the Reno Air Races.

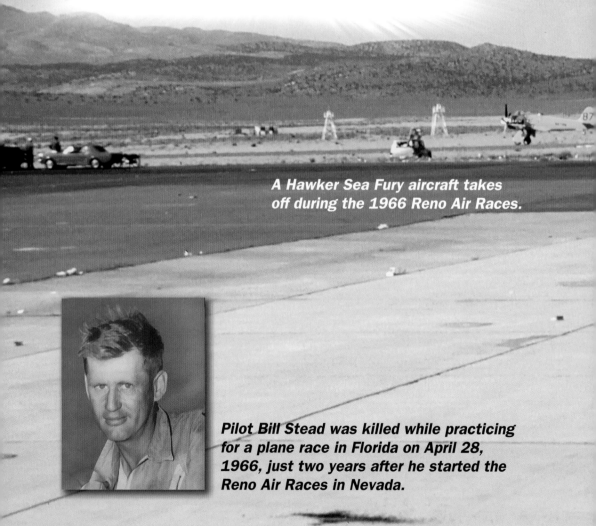

*A Hawker Sea Fury aircraft takes off during the 1966 Reno Air Races.*

*Pilot Bill Stead was killed while practicing for a plane race in Florida on April 28, 1966, just two years after he started the Reno Air Races in Nevada.*

The following year, the races were moved to the Reno-Stead Airport. (The airport was named after Bill's brother, military pilot Croston Stead.) The races have been held there every year since.

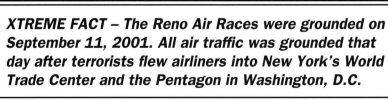

XTREME FACT – The Reno Air Races were grounded on September 11, 2001. All air traffic was grounded that day after terrorists flew airliners into New York's World Trade Center and the Pentagon in Washington, D.C.

# CLASSES

The Reno Air Races include seven classes of planes: Formula One, Biplane, T-6, Sport, Super Sport, Jet, and Unlimited aircraft. Each class competes separately.

*Formula One planes reach speeds of 250 mph (402 kph). They are the smallest planes flown and were once called Midget class.*

*Outrageous - #12*
*Miss Min - #54*

Biplanes are modern planes with an upper and a lower wing. The most common biplane flown in the Reno Air Races is the Pitts S-1S. These biplanes are small. They are well known for aerobatic and sport flying, racing at speeds of 200 mph (322 kph).

*Gone BiListic - #80*

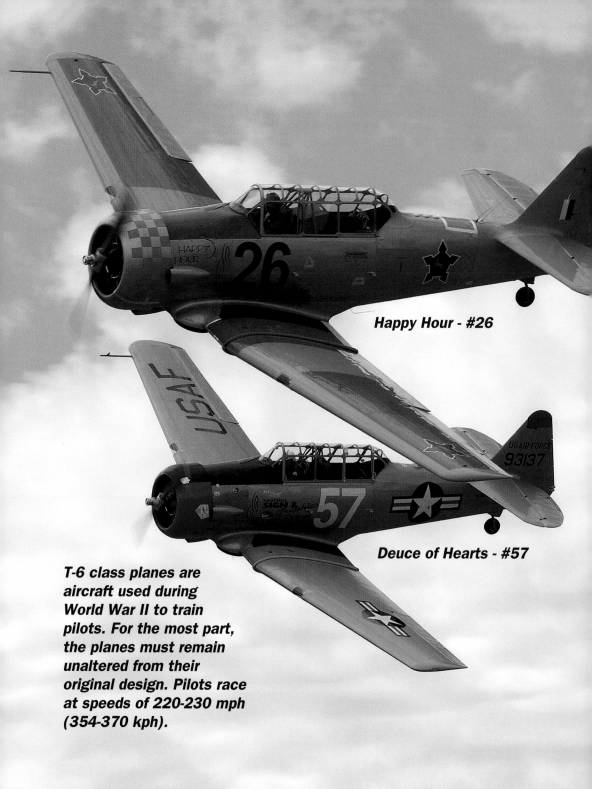

Happy Hour - #26

Deuce of Hearts - #57

T-6 class planes are aircraft used during World War II to train pilots. For the most part, the planes must remain unaltered from their original design. Pilots race at speeds of 220-230 mph (354-370 kph).

Sport class are planes built from kits. Small and fast, they reach speeds of 350 mph (563 kph). The Sport class was introduced in 1998.

*Freedom - #28*
*Sugar Plum - #30*

Super Sport class planes are faster than regular Sport class aircraft, with speeds exceeding 400 mph (644 kph).

*Rapid Travel - #75*

Unlimited class aircraft race at more than 500 mph (805 kph) at a death-defying 50-100 feet (15-30 m) above the ground. Most of the planes are World War II-vintage fighters such as P-51 Mustangs and F4U Corsairs.

*Corsair - #24*

**XTREME FACT –** *The motto for the Reno Air Races is "Fly low, go fast, turn left!"*

*Jet class is the newest entry to the Reno Air Races. Beginning in 2002, Jet class pilots were invited to fly their Czechoslovakian-built Aero Vodochody L-39s. In 2004, any qualified pilot could race in a non-afterburning aircraft. These jets race at speeds of 525 mph (845 kph).*

*Fast Company - #8*

# QUALIFYING

Several days before
the main event, planes
in each class compete
in qualifying matches.
Individually, each
pilot races the
course as fast as
possible. The fastest
qualifiers go on to compete
in the Reno Air Races.
In each class, the
fastest qualifiers fly
against each other in
various races called "heats."
Usually the eight fastest
qualifiers compete in Gold Heats.
The next eight compete in Silver Heats.
And the next eight compete in Bronze Heats.

XTREME FACT – The fastest air racers go two to three times faster than Formula One race cars.

# THE START

A pace plane flies in front of the group of racers. The pilot of the pace plane suddenly veers up out of the way and announces to the racers, "You have a race." The innermost or "pole position" pilot guides the group toward the starting line. Pilots must be extremely careful. They are flying within 50-100 feet (15-30 m) of each other.

A pace plane veers off at the start of a race.

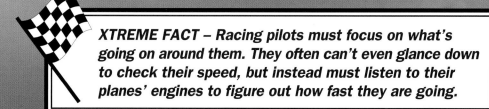

**XTREME FACT** – Racing pilots must focus on what's going on around them. They often can't even glance down to check their speed, but instead must listen to their planes' engines to figure out how fast they are going.

# THE COURSE

Each plane class has a specific course. The shorter courses overlap the longer courses. The planes race around 50-foot (15-m) -high guide pylons. Most of the pylons have bright orange-red panels that can be easily seen by the pilots racing at speeds of up to 500 mph (805 kph). The finish line is marked by a blue-and-white checkered home pylon.

*XTREME FACT – The earliest air race courses were marked with oil drums on top of telephone poles.*

*Happy Hour - #26*

*Eros - #69*

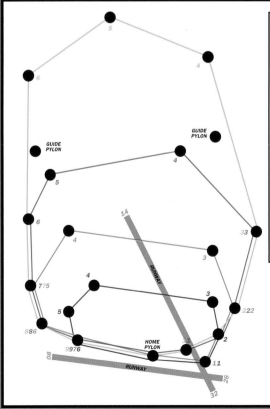

## Reno Air Races Courses

**Unlimited Course: 8.4 miles / 13.5 km**

**Jet Course: 8.5 miles / 13.7 km**

**Sport Course: 8.4 miles / 13.5 km**

**T-6 Course: 5 miles / 8 km**

**Biplane Course: 3.2 miles / 5.1 km**

**Formula One Course: 3.2 miles / 5.1 km**

# THE RULES

After qualifying, the fastest planes fly against each other. Pilots must stay at least 50 feet (15 m) above the ground, but go no higher than 1,500 feet (457 m) in altitude. Pilots must fly outside the course pylons. Pylon judges stand "at the sticks" (pylons) to check every competitor. Judges on the ground look up through the cans as planes fly by. If any part of the plane appears in the hole, it is called a "pylon cut." This is a penalty. At the end of the race, a certain number of seconds are added to the pilot's final time. This can change who wins the race.

# DANGERS

Air racing is dangerous. Planes fly wingtip-to-wingtip at high speeds. Pilots must know the exact size of their plane, the space between planes, and their distance from the ground. From 1964 until 2011, 19 people died while competing in the Reno Air Races. Most were pilots experiencing problems with their planes or misjudging the space between planes or pylons. Winds, such as downdrafts and even a dust devil, also caused accidents.

*In 1979, during the championship race, Steve Hinton lost power and crashed in his RB-51 Red Baron. The plane was destroyed, but Hinton survived the crash. After a long recovery, he continued to fly.*

In 2011, a stalled P-51D Mustang flown by James Leeward crashed into the audience. The pilot and 10 fans were killed. More than 70 people were injured. It was the third-deadliest air show disaster in U.S. history. After the tragedy, the course and pre-race aircraft inspections were modified to add additional safety measures for th

# Top Pilots and Planes

Several pilots have won the Reno Air Show many times. Their flying ability and their ground teams' skills have brought out the best in their planes.

*Pilot Darryl Greenamyer has won in both the Unlimited and Sport class. He and pilot Bill Destefani each have seven wins in the Unlimited class as of 2012.*

*Pilot Jon Sharp has the most Reno Air Show wins as of 2012. Sharp competes in Formula One, Sport, and Super Sport classes. He won the Formula One class for nine consecutive years from 1991-1999.*

*Jon Sharp*

*XTREME FACT – Only pilot Ray Cote has won the Formula One class more times (13 wins) than Jon Sharp (11 wins).*

Eddie Van Fossen

Nick Macy

Pilots Eddie Van Fossen and Nick Macy have the most wins in the T-6 class. Van Fossen won seven times and Macy has won six as of 2012.

Curt Brown is a five-time winner in the Jet class.

Tom Aberle is an eight-time winner in the Biplane class.

# TRADITIONS

## Special performances are conducted by skilled military and civilian pilots at the Reno Air Show.

*The U.S. Navy Blue Angels often perform at the Reno Air Show. This military flight demonstration team flies modified F/A-18 Hornets.*

*The Patriots Jet Team performs high-speed passes and other aerobatic maneuvers in L-39 Albatrosses.*

The U.S. Air Force Thunderbirds perform precise aerial maneuvers in F-16 Fighting Falcons.

Stunt pilot Kent Pietsch entertains air show fans in his 1942 "Jelly Belly" Interstate Cadet.

The Shockwave Jet Truck races airplanes at more than 300 miles per hour (483 kph).

# THE FINISH

Winners of the
Reno Air Races,
in each of the
classes, receive
trophies and prize
money for their
dangerous and
skilled piloting.

NATIONAL
CHAMPIONSHIP AIR RACES
## UNLIMITED GOLD CHAMPION

| YEAR | WINNER | AIRCRAFT | SPEED |
|---|---|---|---|
| 1964 | MIRA SLOVAK | F8F | 366.840 MPH |
| 1965 | DARRYL GREENAMYER | F8F | 375.090 MPH |
| 1966 | DARRYL GREENAMYER | F8F | 396.221 MPH |
| 1967 | DARRYL GREENAMYER | F8F | 392.621 MPH |
| 1968 | DARRYL GREENAMYER | F8F | 388.654 MPH |
| 1969 | DARRYL GREENAMYER | F8F | 412.631 MPH |
| 1970 | CLAY LACY | P51 | 387.342 MPH |
| 1971 | DARRYL GREENAMYER | F8F | 413.987 MPH |
| 1972 | GUNTHER BALZ | P51 | 416.160 MPH |
| 1973 | LYLE SHELTON | F8F | 428.155 MPH |
| 1974 | KEN BURNSTINE | P51 | 381.482 MPH |
| 1975 | LYLE SHELTON | F8F | 429.916 MPH |
| 1976 | LEFTY GARDNER | P51 | 379.610 MPH |
| 1977 | DARRYL GREENAMYER | RB51 | 430.703 MPH |
| 1978 | STEVE HINTON | RB51 | 415.457 MPH |
| 1979 | JOHN CROCKER | P51 | 422.302 MPH |
| 1980 | MAC McCLAIN | P40 | 433.010 MPH |
| 1981 | SKIP HOLM | P40 | 431.288 MPH |
| 1982 | RON HEVLE | P40 | 405.093 MPH |
| 1983 | NEIL ANDERSON | SEA FURY | 425.242 MPH |
| 1984 | SKIP HOLM | P40 | 437.621 MPH |

The winner's trophy features a plane flying over the home pylon. Trophies are awarded in each of the plane classes. The winner's name is engraved on the trophy's base.

# GLOSSARY

### AFTERBURNER

A device on a jet aircraft that injects extra fuel into the engine. This provides extra thrust for supersonic flight. The increased speed comes at the price of consuming much more fuel than normal flight.

### AVIATOR

Another name for a pilot. Usually a person who is exceptionally skilled at flying a plane.

### HEAT

A race or contest between several similarly skilled competitors.

### PACE PLANE

The plane that flies in front of a row of racing planes. The pilot of the pace plane announces the start of the race and then veers off, away from the racers.

### POLE POSITION

In a race, the inside front row position. It is generally thought that the pole position is the best place to start. In the Reno Air Races, the pilot with the fastest qualifying time is given the pole position.

## PYLON

A vertical marking structure that shows a race's path. In an air race, the pylon is a pole with an open barrel on top. Planes must fly completely around the outside of a pylon or face a time penalty.

## QUALIFYING MATCH

An early race where the fastest competitors move on, or qualify, to compete in an actual race.

## WORLD WAR II

A war that was fought from 1939 to 1945, involving countries around the world. The United States entered the war after Japan's bombing of the American naval base at Pearl Harbor, in Oahu, Hawaii, on December 7, 1941.

# INDEX

## A

Aberle, Tom  25
Aero Vodochody L-39  13
Air Force, U.S.  27

## B

Biplane (class)  8, 9, 19, 25
Blue Angels  26
Bronze Heat  14
Brown, Curt  25

## C

Corsair  5, 12
Cote, Ray  24

## D

Destefani, Bill  24

## F

F4U Corsair  12
F-16 Fighting Falcon  27
F/A-18 Hornet  26
Florida  6
Formula One (class)  8, 19, 24
Formula One race car  15

## G

Gold Heat  14
Greenamyer, Darryl  24

## H

Hawker Sea Fury  6
Hinton, Steve  22

## I

Interstate Cadet  27

## J

Jelly Belly Interstate Cadet  27
Jet (class)  8, 13, 19, 25

## L

L-39 Albatross  13, 26
Leeward, James  23

## M

Macy, Nick  25
Midget (class)  8
Mustang  12, 23

## N

National Championship Air Races  4
Navy, U.S.  26
Nevada  4, 6
New York, NY  7

## P

P-51 Mustang  12, 23
pace plane  16, 17
Patriots Jet Team  26
Pentagon  7
Pietsch, Kent  27
Pitts S-1S  9
pole position  16
pylon  5, 18, 20, 22, 29

## R

RB-51 Red Baron  22
Reno, NV  6
Reno-Stead Airport  7

## S

Sharp, Jon  24
Shockwave Jet Truck  27
Silver Heat  14
Sky Ranch Airfield  6
Sport (class) 8, 11, 19, 24
Stead, Bill  6, 7
Stead, Croston  7
Super Sport (class)  8, 11, 24

## T

T-6 (class)  8, 10, 19, 25
Thunderbirds  27

## U

United States  23, 26, 27
Unlimited (class)  8, 12, 19, 24

## V

Van Fossen, Eddie  25

## W

Washington, D.C.  7
World Trade Center  7
World War II  10, 12
World's Fastest Motorsport, The  4